Grace Ledden, MA,

Watch me bloom
when I have big feelings

Watch me bloom when I have big feelings

A coping story for children with autism on how to manage emotions, practice social skills and navigate big feelings.

Written by Grace Ledden, MA, BCBA
Illustrated by CyAn Platas

Paperback edition   ISBN: 978-1-962410-00-7
Digital edition   ISBN: 978-1-962410-01-4

Published by Daily Bloom LLC - Tennessee, USA

www.mydailybloom.com

To all the families who walk the unique path of autism.

This book is dedicated to you, in recognition of the journey you embark on every day. May it serve as a small reminder that you are seen, you are loved, and you are not alone. Here's to the extraordinary lives that you lead, and the stories you continue to write every day.

This book belongs to

_____

Hello, my friend! My name is Noah, and I am unique too. I have autism, but that does not stop me from playing, learning, and exploring.

Sometimes I have big feelings, and I get overwhelmed, upset, and even angry.

One day, I was building a tall tower with my blocks. I stacked my blocks one on top of the other, trying to build a tower that touched the ceiling. But no matter how hard I tried, my tower kept falling down.

My hands were shaking, and I could feel tears in my eyes. I was so upset that my tower wasn't turning out the way I wanted it to. I felt pressure build inside my chest like a storm was starting to rage inside of me. I didn't know what to do.

Just then I felt a gentle tap on my shoulder. I turned around and could not believe my eyes – in front of me stood a small gnome with big blue eyes and a pointy green hat. I could have sworn he wasn't there two seconds ago...

"Hello, Noah," he said. "My name is Bud and I am your Bloom Buddy."

I wasn't sure what to say to him. I had never met a Bloom Buddy before.

"I see you are upset and that's okay" he said. "Everyone feels upset or angry sometimes, even me."

"Really?" I asked as I looked down at my chest, wondering if he could see the storm inside me.

"Sure, Noah. Let me show you what I do when I get upset," said Bud.

"Noah, when I feel upset, I want to cry or scream too. Instead, I squeeze my hands and count to 3. Then I take a deep breath in and breathe out, blowing all my upset feelings away. I do this until I feel better."

Bud squeezed his hands for 3 seconds and took a slow and steady deep breath in. He held his breath for a moment before gently blowing it out.

"Let's practice together," said Bud.

I squeezed my hands for 3 seconds and took a slow deep breath in, just like Bud had. I breathed out, gently pushing the storm out of my chest and away from me. It worked. My upset feelings were gone!

I felt better and I could keep playing with my blocks. I went back to stacking them one on top of the other and this time my tower almost touched the ceiling!

"Good job, Noah," said Bud. "Remember, it's okay to feel upset. If you ever need me again, think of me, and I will be here to help you."

With that, Bud disappeared in a shower of shimmering sparkles.

On the weekend, I met my friends at the park to play. We were running around, laughing, and having fun together. But soon, everyone started to get really loud.

I put my hands over my ears, but the noise was still too loud for me. It rumbled in my ears so loudly that it sounded like an airplane was taking off inside my head. I started to get angry and upset as the sound overwhelmed me. My friends were too loud and I wanted them to stop.

Just when I thought that these big feelings would make my head explode, I felt a tap on my shoulder.

"Hello again, Noah," Bud said with a big smile. "Are you okay? Seems like it's a bit noisy for you here?"

I was too overwhelmed to reply to him as I sat there with my hands over my ears, so I simply shook my head.

"When the other Bloom Buddies are getting too loud, I use my words to say how I feel," said Bud. "If a friend is being too loud, you can say 'quiet please' or 'stop please'. You can also ask for some space or ask to leave the room."

I nodded my head. This sounded like a good idea, but more than anything I just needed the noise to stop.

"Let's practice together," said Bud.

"Quiet please!" I said to my friends.

It worked! My friends were still laughing and playing, but they were not as loud. I took my hands off my ears. I was not feeling upset anymore and was ready to go play with my friends again.

"Good job, Noah," said Bud. "Remember, it's okay to feel upset when friends are loud. Just use your words and say 'quiet please' or you can ask for some space. If you ever need me again, think of me, and I will be here to help you."

And with that Bud disappeared once more into a shower of shimmering sparkles.

Yesterday, I was watching TV when my baby sister started to cry. She was hungry, and her cries were very loud.

I put my hands over my ears, but her crying was still too loud for me. Even with my hands over my ears, it felt like a siren blaring in my head.

I felt upset and wished I could make it stop.

Just as I was about to have really big feelings, I remembered Bud's advice and tried to use my words.

"Quiet please," I said to my baby sister.

"Quiet please," I said again with my hands over my ears.

"Quiet please!" I said to my sister, but she would not stop crying.

It was not working, and the crying was getting louder. She must have been very hungry. I guess she is too little to understand, "quiet please".

"Mom, it's hurting my ears! I need space. Can I go to my room, please?" I asked.

"Of course, Noah," Mom said. "I'm proud of you for using your words while you are having such big feelings. Head on up to your room. She will be quiet soon once she has her bottle."

I went to my room for some space just like Bud told me to.

I remembered how Bud had taught me to breathe out my big feelings.

I squeezed my hands for 3 seconds, took a deep breath in, and blew away my upset feelings.

It worked! I did not feel as upset anymore. I felt so much better that I was ready to go back and see my baby sister.

Just then Bud appeared in a brilliant burst of shimmering sparkles.

"Good job, Noah," said Bud. "You didn't need me this time. You remembered to use your words and say 'quiet please', you also asked Mom for space and on top of all that, you remembered to blow your upset feelings away!"

Bud smiled up at me and I smiled back.

"I'm so proud of you, Noah. You have learned so much so quickly. You are doing a great job. I'll see you soon on our next adventure together."

And with that Bud disappeared once more into a shower of shimmering sparkles, but I knew I would see him again soon.

Watch Your Child Bloom with More Daily Bloom Coping Stories!

Help Me Grow - Share Your Feedback!

As an independent author, your review makes a big difference. It helps me reach new readers and continue creating stories that enrich little ones' lives.

Please scan the QR code below to leave a review and discover more from Daily Bloom.

As a thank you, you can also download exclusive content featuring the Bloom Buddies!

PRIVACY.FLOWCODE.COM

About the Author

Grace Ledden, MA, BCBA, is a Board Certified Behavior Analyst specializing in creating individualized support and treatment for young children diagnosed with autism and their families. Grace graduated with a Master's degree in Applied Behavior Analysis with an emphasis in autism. Grace seeks to create visual supports and tools that will help young children and their families navigate their world and lead a more meaningful life. Grace strives to be part of creating a world that is more inclusive, accepting, and understanding of neurodiversity.

Thank you for choosing to share "Watch me bloom when I have big feelings" with your child.

My hope for this series was to offer our young readers a mirror, reflecting their experiences and feelings, while also empowering them with tangible strategies and techniques. By understanding, managing, and expressing their feelings, they can build a foundation of emotional resilience and self-awareness.

This story highlights different challenges Noah faces in processing sensory inputs and emotions. With Bud always appearing when Noah needs guidance the most, creates a sense of security and reassurance. Noah not only learns to manage his emotions but also communicates effectively with those around him.

It's like planting a seed that will eventually grow into a sturdy tree, capable of withstanding life's storms. By giving children a language to talk about their emotions and strategies to cope with them, we're giving them a lifelong gift.

- Grace Ledden

More ways to bloom beyond big feelings